Walt Disney's
MINNIE MYSTERIES
The Noisy Attic

By Catherine Hapka

Illustrated by DiCicco Digital Arts

A GOLDEN BOOK • NEW YORK

Golden Books Publishing Company, Inc., New York, New York 10106

"Isn't this a super movie, Minnie?" Daisy Duck whispered.

Minnie Mouse peeked at her friend. "It's sort of spooky," she whispered back.

"It's supposed to be spooky, silly," Daisy said. "It's a ghost story."

Minnie headed straight home after the movie. She was still a little scared. The moonlight cast an eerie-looking shadow across the room. And Minnie noticed her floor creaking. Finally, when the rain started to splash against the window, Minnie jumped.

Minnie felt better once she climbed into her cozy bed. But just as she was drifting off to sleep she heard a sudden noise from above. *THUMP! THUMP!* it went.

Minnie sat up, shuddering. "W-w-what was that?" she whispered to her cat, Fluffy.

Minnie and Fluffy stared up at the ceiling. There were no more thumps. Instead, Minnie heard a strange skittering noise. It reminded her of the ghost in the movie clanking his chains!

"I have to see what's making that noise," Minnie said bravely. She climbed out of bed and crept toward the attic stairs. As she climbed, the sounds got louder. Minnie shivered with fear.

Minnie reached the top step and took a deep breath.
"Who's there?" she shouted, trying to sound brave.

The noises stopped.

Minnie gulped. She pushed the door open and
stepped into the attic.

No one was there.

What made those strange sounds? Minnie wondered.

Suddenly, Minnie caught sight of a reflection in an old mirror. Something white and wispy fluttered by—*right behind Minnie!*

She whirled around, her heart pounding harder than ever. But nothing was there.

Minnie took a deep breath and raced for the door.

Once Minnie was safely downstairs, she began to wonder if she had imagined the spooky sounds and the ghostly image. But before long, the strange noises started again.

Then the lights began to flicker! "Oh, no!" Minnie gasped. She raced back to her bedroom. "What if the ghost makes the lights go out?" she said to Fluffy as she hugged her tightly.

"I've got to put a stop to this!" Minnie exclaimed as she headed back toward the attic. This time Fluffy followed.

"Go away, ghosts!" Minnie cried. She flung the door open. Again, the attic was as quiet and as still as could be . . . until suddenly, there was a small skittering sound!

Minnie jumped in fear, only to find Fluffy batting a small toy across the floor. Minnie grabbed the cat and the toy and raced for the stairs. All she wanted was to escape from her haunted attic.

As soon as Minnie climbed into bed, the ghostly noises began again. But with Fluffy purring loudly in her ear, Minnie finally fell asleep.

The next morning, Minnie could still hear the strange sounds, which didn't
seem quite so scary in the daylight. All the same, she decided to call her
friend Daisy to see if she could come over.

"Of course," said Daisy. "I'll be right there." Within minutes she was at
Minnie's door.

"Come with me," Minnie said. She led Daisy upstairs. "Do you hear that?"
Daisy listened. "It does sound kind of spooky," she said.

Minnie told Daisy the whole story. "First the sounds started," she said. "Then I saw a ghostly form in the mirror. And after that, the lights flickered."

"Well," said Daisy, "I think I can explain the lights flickering. Mine did, too. That was because of the storm."

"Oh, of course," said Minnie as Fluffy rubbed against her legs. Suddenly, Minnie remembered the toy. It was in her pocket.

"What's that?" Daisy asked as Minnie pulled it out.

Minnie stared at Fluffy's toy. "An acorn," she said slowly. "Hmm. Maybe we can catch my ghost after all."

Minnie waved for Daisy to follow as she crept silently up the attic stairs. The skittering noises continued.

When she reached the door, Minnie was careful not to make a sound. She reached for the knob . . . turned it quietly . . . flung the door open—and caught a pair of very startled squirrels gnawing on acorns in the middle of the floor!

"What you heard was snacking squirrels coming in out of the rain," said Daisy. "Your house isn't haunted after all."

"Thanks to Fluffy, I finally figured that out!" said Minnie.

The intruders scampered out the window, and Minnie noticed the curtains blowing in the breeze. The fluttering fabric was reflected in the mirror. "That's the ghost I saw last night!" she cried.

"And that must be the thumping sound!" Daisy said with a giggle. The wind was blowing the shutters open and shut.

Minnie closed the window. "Sorry, squirrels!" she said. "This should keep you out." Minnie smiled. "Who knows? It might even keep out a few ghosts, too!"